HOW
MR. DOG
GOT TAME

Printed in Canada

ISBN 0-8167-4350-9

10 9 8 7 6 5 4 3 2   Designed by Susan and Dave Albers

LEGENDS OF THE WORLD

HOW MR. DOG GOT TAME

AN AFRICAN-AMERICAN LEGEND

RETOLD BY JANET P. JOHNSON   ILLUSTRATED BY CHARLES REASONER

Troll

Everyone knows that Mr. Dog is almost everybody's best friend. Just take a look around you. Mr. Dog is helping the farmer round up the sheep. Mr. Dog is helping to guard the house. And if you're a young boy or girl, you know best of all what a friend Mr. Dog can be—especially when it's time to clean your plate of all the things you don't like!

But here's something you might not know. Mr. Dog was not always such a fine friend to you and me. Long ago, he was just as wild as Mr. Wolf and Mr. Fox and Mr. Raccoon.

In those days, Mr. Dog liked to roam wild. He ran free as a breeze through the forest, sniffing the air. He usually traveled with a pack of other dogs, just as natural as can be. At that time, Mr. Dog was friends with many of the other wild animals.

Sometimes he'd go hunting with Mr. Wolf. Other times, he might carry on with Mr. Fox. At night, he liked to prowl with Mr. Raccoon. And Mr. Dog lived outside all year long. He had one rule, and one rule only: Never get too close to a man, woman, or child.

Most times, things were good, and Mr. Dog liked his life just fine. But other times, things weren't so good.

One hard winter, the winds howled loud, long, and cold. Mr. Dog and his friends had nowhere to go to get warm. One day, they ran into a cave where Mr. Bear was sleeping. But it turned out that Mr. Bear was a light sleeper and didn't want any company. Mr. Dog and his friends had to get out of there fast!

The days got colder, and the snow got deeper. Food was getting hard to find. Mr. Dog went hunting, but he came up empty-handed. Most of the birds had flown south. The rabbits had turned white as the snow and couldn't be found.

The chipmunks were hiding, warm beneath the ground. And the squirrels were cuddled up together inside their nests in the trees.

Mr. Dog hadn't eaten a meal in so many days, he felt mighty weak. He curled up in the snow and tried to sleep.

But before his eyes had closed, Mr. Dog heard howling. This time it wasn't the wind. It was his old friend Mr. Wolf. Mr. Wolf trotted up, took one look at Mr. Dog, and said, "Your ribs look ready to poke holes in your sides."

"You're right about that," replied Mr. Dog. "But the growls coming from your stomach are just about the fiercest sound in the forest."

"Sure and certain," agreed Mr. Wolf. "I wish we could find something to eat. If we don't, what's to become of us?"

Mr. Dog didn't know the answer to that question, so he just curled up tighter in the snow.

Suddenly, Mr. Wolf's eyes lit up. "I know what we need," he said. "We need to get ourselves a nice chunk of fire."

"Fire?" asked Mr. Dog.

"Yes," insisted Mr. Wolf. "With that bit of fire, we'll be ready to cook the first thing we find. If we don't find anything to eat, at least we can warm ourselves and not freeze in the snow."

It all made sense to Mr. Dog. But where would they get some fire?

Mr. Wolf had the answer to that one, too. "One of us has got to pay a visit to Mr. Man and Mrs. Woman. I heard they've got plenty of fire in the house where they live."

But neither Mr. Dog nor Mr. Wolf was too eager to go see Mr. Man and Mrs. Woman. It was known among the wild animals that those folks owned a special stick that could explode in your face!

Finally, Mr. Dog was shivering so much, he couldn't stand it anymore. "I'll go and see about the fire," he said.

"Bring it right back," said Mr. Wolf.

"Sure thing," said Mr. Dog.

He set off.

The next afternoon he crept up quietly to the house of
Mr. Man and Mrs. Woman. First, he went to the front door,
but that seemed too scary. So he went round to the back.
Through the fence he heard children laughing. It was a
happy-sounding noise. For the first time in his life, Mr. Dog
felt lonely. He sniffed the air. Sure enough, he smelled smoke
from the fire. It was coming out of the chimney of the little
house.

But that wasn't the only thing Mr. Dog smelled. Fresh-roasting ham filled the air with a delicious aroma. And baking cornbread didn't smell bad either!

Mr. Dog was scared about being so close to the house. He wanted to run away. But those good smells kept him right where he was. He lay down on the ground and breathed them in. Little dribble-drools ran out of his mouth, and he whined just a bit before he knew what he was doing.

One of the children heard the sound and looked outside and over the fence. Then she ran through the house, calling, "Daddy! Come and see who I found!"

Mr. Dog shivered and shook, as much from fright as from the cold, but still he didn't move. The door opened and out came Mr. Man, carrying his special stick. He looked at Mr. Dog, lying on the ground with his head down. "Get out of here," said Mr. Man. "Quick!"

But Mr. Dog was so cold and scared, he couldn't move. Instead, his tail started wagging. The door opened again, and Mrs. Woman came out. "Who's this?" she asked.

"It's a dog," said Mr. Man. "And he's up to no good."

Mrs. Woman took a look at the shivering creature. Mr. Dog got up his courage and looked at Mrs. Woman with his big, brown eyes. Those eyes were so pitiful and sad that Mrs. Woman said, "He doesn't seem as if he's up to no good. What do you want, Mr. Dog?"

"I came to see if I could borrow a little chunk of fire from you," said Mr. Dog.

"Why? Are you planning to burn down the forest?" asked Mr. Man suspiciously.

"No," answered Mr. Dog. "I just want to cook some food and stay warm."

"You poor thing," said Mrs. Woman. "Come in by the fire and get warm. But after that you'll have to get going."

"Thank you, ma'am," answered Mr. Dog.

Inside the house, it was like a little bit of heaven. That fire felt so good, Mr. Dog got too close and almost singed his hide. The children ran around the kitchen, tossing a ball. Soon Mr. Dog was playing a game with them. Best of all, he was closer than ever to those delicious smells.

When it came time for dinner, Mr. Dog wanted to ask for some grub, but he was too shy. So he sat by the fire, quiet as could be.

"What a good dog," said Mrs. Woman. She filled a plate with ham and cornbread for him. Mr. Dog gobbled it up. He could have eaten more, but he waited politely until the family gave him scraps from their plates.

Meanwhile, it had started to snow real hard. When it came time for Mr. Dog to go, the children begged, "Please let him stay! Just for tonight!"

And so Mr. Dog spent his first night inside a house. He had to admit it was mighty comfortable. The next morning, Mr. Dog played with the children. Mrs. Woman fed him porridge and milk. Then Mr. Dog went out with Mr. Man. Soon he was helping the farmer round up the sheep and the cows. Later, they went hunting. Mr. Dog's fine nose and Mr. Man's exploding stick made quite a handy combination.

One day led to the next, and Mr. Dog settled right in without a bit of trouble. He got along fine with everyone, and they liked him a lot, too.

But one day, while he was out in the forest taking a walk, Mr. Dog ran into his old friend Mr. Wolf. "Whatever happened to you the day you went to get the fire?" asked Mr. Wolf.

"A mighty strange thing," Mr. Dog replied. He told his friend all about life at the farmer's house. "It's too good to leave," concluded Mr. Dog.

It sounded pretty good to Mr. Wolf, too. "Do you suppose they might invite me in?" he asked.

"I don't see why not," answered Mr. Dog.

So that night, Mr. Wolf went creeping up to the front door of the little house in the forest. But Mr. Dog didn't know it was Mr. Wolf who had come to call. When he heard a sound outside, he let out a warning growl. In a flash, Mr. Man had his exploding stick ready. He rushed out the door—and ran straight into Mr. Wolf. That gave him quite a fright! "What are you doing here?" yelled the man.

Mr. Wolf was scared, too. Instead of answering, he tried to show what a friendly, polite animal he could be. He smiled as big a smile as he could. But to Mr. Man, all those sharp, white teeth looked anything but friendly!

Mr. Man raised his stick and fired. Lucky for Mr. Wolf, he was already hightailing it out of there. He disappeared into the dark night and didn't come back. To this day, Mr. Wolf still wonders what he did wrong.

And to this day, Mr. Dog and Mr. Man, Mrs. Woman, and their children are living together as happily as ever. But, of course, you and I know it wasn't always so. For now you know the story of how Mr. Dog got tame!

From the 1500s to the 1800s, great numbers of West Africans were captured and taken to the West Indies and to the Americas by slave traders. It is in this period of time that African-American folklore and tradition have their beginnings. For in moving from their homeland to America, the slaves brought their African

heritage with them. Because attempts by the black population to maintain its culture were punished by slave owners, certain aspects of the original customs changed over time. For example, slaves were not allowed to play their native music, yet the African musical style remained with the slaves. By creating new compositions, African-Americans forged a new music, which is one element of African-American culture. In addition, a beautiful form of music called jazz grew out of this blending of two cultures.

Folktales—stories told by word of mouth from one generation to the next—are another important part of African-American culture. The stories told by the slaves often had their roots in African tales. Because the slaves were prohibited from reading and writing, these stories were never written down. One of the first authors to do so was Joel Chandler Harris. This white newspaperman realized the rich literary treasure to be found in black folktales. His many collections of stories, including a version of *How Mr. Dog Got Tame*, are told by the fictional character of Uncle Remus, a former slave. Many find Uncle Remus to be a controversial character because he spoke fondly about slavery. Despite the controversy over Uncle Remus, Harris's contribution to literature remains a major one because it preserves so much African-American folklore.

How Mr. Dog Got Tame is an example of a "why" tale. Such folk legends, which are found in many cultures, seek to explain why certain conditions exist in nature or among animals and people. With its wise view of human nature, *Mr. Dog* is a wonderful example of African-American storytelling.